The Boxcar Children Mysteries

THE MYSTERY IN THE FORTUNE COOKIE

created by
GERTRUDE CHANDLER WARNER

Illustrated by Hodges Soileau

SCHOLASTIC INC.
New York Toronto London Auckland Sydney
New Delhi Mexico City Hong Kong Buenos Aires

ISBN 0-439-51749-4

12 11 10 9 8 7 6 5 4 3   3 4 5 6 7 8/0

Printed in the U.S.A.   40
First Scholastic printing, September 2003

Contents

CHAPTER 1

The Underground

"Hurry, Jessie!" cried six-year-old Benny. "There won't be any fortune cookies left if we don't hurry." The youngest Alden was bouncing up and down with excitement on Aunt Jane's couch.

Twelve-year-old Jessie looked up from the gift she was wrapping. "Oh, Benny," she said, smiling over at her little brother. "The Kowloon Restaurant *never* runs out of fortune cookies."

The Alden children — Henry, Jessie, Violet, and Benny — were staying with their

Aunt Jane for a week to keep her company while Uncle Andy was away on business. The Aldens were looking forward to a special Chinese dinner that night in downtown Elmford. They were going to the Kowloon Restaurant with Aunt Jane and her friends Dottie and Martin. The dinner was a celebration of Dottie's birthday. The Kowloon Restaurant was Dottie's favorite place to eat.

Jessie was wearing her best honey-colored dress. Violet had changed into her frilly lavender skirt and a white shirt. Henry wore a navy blazer and light blue trousers. And Benny had on a silver-gray blazer over his favorite red shirt and charcoal trousers.

"I hope Dottie likes our gift," said ten-year-old Violet, clasping her hands.

"I'm sure she'll like it," Henry assured her. "It's the perfect present for Dottie." At fourteen, Henry was the oldest of the Aldens.

Jessie nodded. "A framed picture of The Underground really *is* just the right gift for Dottie." The Underground was the name of the bookstore that Dottie Shallum owned with her business partner, Martin Howard. Dottie and Martin shared a fondness for old and rare books. The Underground sold lots of them.

Jessie glanced admiringly at her younger sister, who had taken the picture. "You're a wonderful photographer, Violet."

"Thanks, Jessie." Violet smiled gratefully. "I think I *am* getting better at taking pictures. But I still have a lot to learn," she added modestly. Photography was one of Violet's hobbies. She often took her camera along when the Aldens went on vacation.

Jessie added one last pink bow to their gift. "Aunt Jane chose just the right frame for it, too. The dark wood matches the bookshelves in The Underground."

Aunt Jane smiled broadly at her nieces and nephews as she came down the stairs. She was wearing a pale blue dress and matching shoes. "Are we ready to get this show on the road?" she asked.

Without a moment's pause, the four children cried, "Ready!"

The Aldens piled into Aunt Jane's car and

fastened their seat belts. Soon they were driving through the peaceful countryside toward the small town of Elmford. In almost no time at all, they were pulling into the parking lot near Main Street.

When Benny jumped out of the car, he was still thinking about fortune cookies. "I can't wait to see what my fortune will say!" He sounded excited. "I like opening fortune cookies almost as much as I like eating them!"

Benny loved fortune cookies. Each crunchy, bow-shaped cookie had a fortune hidden inside, neatly typed on little white slips of paper. Benny kept a whole collection of the fortunes in an old sock. He'd even brought the collection with him to Aunt Jane's.

"I bet my fortune says a mystery's coming our way!" Benny went on.

"Oh, Benny," said Jessie, shaking her head and laughing. "Mysteries are *always* coming our way."

The Alden children loved mysteries. Together they'd managed to solve quite a few.

"Fortune cookies can't really tell you anything about the future, Benny. They're just for fun." Henry sounded very sure.

Benny turned to his older brother in surprise. "But some of the fortunes in my collection came true," he protested as they walked along the sidewalk. "Once I got one that said: *A busy week is coming your way.* And guess what. We really *did* have a busy week!"

"But — " began Henry.

"And you know what else?" Benny cut in, his eyes wide.

"What?" asked Henry, hiding a smile.

"Another one said: *A pleasant surprise is waiting for you.* And the very next day it stopped raining and we had a picnic in the park. Well, that *was* a pleasant surprise."

Henry shook his head. "That was just a coincidence."

Jessie was quick to agree. "Benny, we're *always* busy."

"And thanks to Grandfather," added Violet, "our lives are filled with pleasant surprises."

After their parents died, Jessie, Henry, Benny, and Violet had run away. When they stumbled across an abandoned boxcar in the woods, they made it their home. Then Grandfather found them and brought his grandchildren to live with him in his big white house in Greenfield. He even gave the boxcar a special place in the backyard. The children often used their former home as a clubhouse.

"Do you think Grandfather is lonely this week without us?" kindhearted Violet couldn't help wondering.

"I'm sure Grandfather misses us," Jessie said after a moment's thought. "But don't forget," she reminded Violet, "Mrs. McGregor is there to keep him company." Mrs. McGregor was the Aldens' housekeeper and a wonderful cook.

"And Watch is there, too!" added Benny. Watch was the family dog.

"Well, it's a treat for *me* to have you here," said Aunt Jane. "Look, we've reached The Underground!"

"I love the way the little bookstore is

tucked away like that," Jessie remarked, putting a hand up to shade her eyes. "Right beneath the Big Top T-Shirt Shop, I mean."

"I guess that's why they named it The Underground," Henry realized.

Benny frowned. He was still wondering if fortune cookies really *could* tell anything about the future.

Aunt Jane seemed to read Benny's mind. "Don't worry. It'll still be fun reading our fortunes." She put an arm around her youngest nephew. "*Nobody* knows what tomorrow will bring," she added. "I'm afraid that's always a mystery. But the mystery is part of the fun!"

Benny brightened. "Mysteries *are* fun!"

The children followed Aunt Jane down the stone steps that led to The Underground. At the bottom of the steps was a heavy glass door with the names Dottie Shallum and Martin Howard printed on it in shiny gold script. As the Aldens and Aunt Jane stepped inside the little shop, they breathed in the musty smell of old books.

Dottie and Martin looked up from behind the counter and waved cheerfully. Dottie was tall and slim, with dark, curly hair streaked with gray. Martin was short and round, with a carefully trimmed white mustache. They were both about Grandfather's age.

Benny sprang forward. "Happy birthday, Dottie!" he cried, and the other Aldens echoed his words.

"And we wish you many more to come," added Aunt Jane as Benny handed Dottie their special gift.

Dottie put a hand to her cheek. "Oh, you shouldn't have!" Her eyes were shining as she looked at each of them in turn.

"We like giving presents," Benny told her. Then he quickly added, "But it's okay if you don't open it right now. You might want to eat first."

Jessie smiled at her little brother and brushed her hand across his hair. "Don't worry, Benny. We'll have dinner soon."

"It can't be soon enough for me," put in Martin. "My mouth is watering just thinking about Auntie Two's Chinese food."

Auntie Two was the owner of the Kowloon Restaurant and a friend of Martin and Dottie's.

"I'll second that!" Aunt Jane said.

"That settles it then," declared Dottie. "I'll open my gift at the restaurant — while we're waiting for our food to arrive."

Benny beamed.

Martin took a quick glance at his watch and frowned. "I'm afraid we're stuck here for a moment or two," he told them. "We have a straggler."

"What's a straggler?" Benny wanted to know.

Martin tugged impatiently on his brightly flowered tie. "A customer who lingers long after the others have gone," he muttered under his breath.

The Aldens and Aunt Jane looked at Martin, then in the direction he was staring. Sure enough, a customer was standing in a far corner, half-hidden in the shadows.

"Maybe I can hurry him along," Martin said. Then, clearing his throat, he called out, "Sorry, sir, but those particular books are for display only!"

The customer didn't seem to hear what Martin had said. The man's hands were behind his back, and his legs were wide apart. He appeared to be deep in thought as he stared at the old books inside a cabinet with shiny glass doors. Then, as if feeling everyone's eyes on him, he suddenly looked over.

"What was that?" he asked.

"Just thought I'd mention, the books in that cabinet are for display only."

The man looked startled. "But . . . I'm quite interested in these — " he began. Then he suddenly laughed. "Oh, I get it. You're trying to say — "

"That those books are *not* for sale," finished Martin. "I'm sorry."

The smartly dressed, dark-haired young man stepped out of the shadows. He did not seem to be a bit bothered by this remark. "Unless the price is right, of course," he said, as if he didn't quite believe Martin. An amused smile curled his lips. "Isn't that what you're saying?" Then he raised an eyebrow and jingled the change in his pocket.

"Not everything in this store has a price tag," Dottie interrupted icily. "Some books I would never part with — for *any* price."

"Why not? You mean, because of that mysterious disappearance?" The young man shot Dottie a disbelieving glance. "Surely you don't think it adds to the value of those books, do you?" He waved that away. "That's old news. I'm afraid nobody cares anymore. No, the truth is, those books aren't worth the paper they're printed on."

That was the wrong thing to say. Jessie noticed Martin's whole face suddenly change. His mouth was set in a thin, hard line. He looked like a different person.

"That's enough!" Martin burst out. "Now you really *have* overstayed your welcome, young man." Folding his arms in front of him, Martin jerked his head in the direction of the door. "You know the way out."

Everyone seemed surprised by Martin's harsh tone. Jessie and Henry exchanged a look. They knew Dottie and Martin often bargained with customers over the price of a book. They said it was just part of the business. Why were they getting so upset?

The young man lifted one shoulder in a shrug and turned on his heel. With a few quick strides, he reached the door and was gone.

Henry fixed his gaze on the cabinet in the far corner. He couldn't help thinking that something very odd was going on. Why was Martin so touchy about those books? And what did the customer mean about a mysterious disappearance?

CHAPTER 2

Two Desserts

As they walked over to the Kowloon Restaurant, the Aldens soon forgot about the strange incident at The Underground. Martin, who was back to his usual cheery self, was telling them all about fortune cookies.

"The funny thing is," he was saying as they went inside the restaurant, "most people think fortune cookies were invented in China. But you know something? Until recently, they were almost unknown there."

Everyone looked surprised to hear this.

"Then who came up with the idea?" Benny wanted to know.

"Where *were* they invented?" Henry said at the same time.

"Right here in America," Martin answered. He led the way to an empty table by the window.

A young woman in a white apron came over to greet them. She was tall and slender, with thick copper-red hair that hung down to her waist. "Welcome to the Kowloon Restaurant!" she said with a friendly smile. "My name's Lucy Monroe. Auntie Two hired me to help out for the summer," she added after everyone had introduced themselves. "I'll be working here until college starts again in the fall."

Jessie smiled as the waitress handed out the menus. "What are you studying at school?"

"I'm in the creative writing program," said Lucy. Then she leaned forward as if about to share a secret. "Inventing stories has always been a great hobby of mine." Just then, she noticed someone waiting to be seated and hurried away.

Everyone was quiet as they looked over the menus carefully. Each of them decided to order something different and share with the others. That way they could sample many dishes. Lucy returned and they ordered wonton soup, egg rolls, lemon chicken, chow mein, sweet-and-sour spare ribs, chop suey, and pork fried rice.

While they waited for their food, Dottie turned her attention to her birthday present. She quickly tore away the pink and gold wrapping. When she caught sight of the framed photograph, she laughed and clapped her hands. "What a wonderful surprise!"

Violet let out the breath she'd been holding.

"Violet took the picture herself," Benny told Dottie. "She's a very good photographer," he added proudly.

Martin was quick to agree. "You've captured all the charm of our little bookstore, Violet. You're becoming quite a pro."

A flush of crimson crept across Violet's face. "Thank you," she said with a shy smile.

When their drinks arrived, Martin said, "I believe I ordered a cola, Lucy, not an iced tea."

"Oh, I'm so sorry!" Lucy slapped a hand against her cheek. "I'm always getting orders mixed up. Will I ever learn?"

Aunt Jane smiled warmly. "Don't worry. We won't hold it against you."

When Lucy had gone, Martin reached into his jacket pocket and removed an envelope. "Just a little something," he said, holding it out to Dottie. "Happy birthday."

Dottie looked surprised — and pleased. "How thoughtful, Martin!" She opened the flap of the envelope and pulled out a heart-shaped birthday card. Inside were two tickets for the Friday night symphony concert. Dottie read the words on the card aloud: " 'To Dorothy Ruth Ursela May — Enjoy the concert! Love, Martin.' "

"I happen to be free Friday night," Martin pointed out. "If you're wondering what to do with one of those tickets, I mean."

With a teasing twinkle in her eye, Dottie said, "I'll keep that in mind, Martin."

Violet and Jessie glanced at each other. They wondered if Martin had a crush on Dottie.

"There's something I don't understand," Benny said as the soup was put in front of them. "Why are there only two tickets to the concert? What about all those other people?"

Dottie looked confused. "What other people, Benny?"

"Ruth, Ursela, and May."

The corners of Dottie's mouth began to twitch and then she laughed. "That's me, Benny," she said. "*I'm* Dorothy Ruth Ursela May." When she saw the look of surprise on the children's faces, she explained. "You see, my parents couldn't decide which of four names to give me. So they just—"

"Gave you all four names?" guessed Henry.

"That's exactly what they did, Henry," said Dottie. "Of course, folks in Elmford just call me Dottie."

Martin put down his soup spoon. "I re-member when you first arrived in town," he said, giving Dottie a meaningful look. "That was my lucky day."

Dottie sighed a little. "I can't believe how the years have flown by since I left Keller's Crossing." She turned to Aunt Jane and the Aldens. "It was just after my husband died. That's when I packed up my bags and left my hometown for good."

None of the Aldens liked to hear the note of sadness in their good friend's voice. As the soup bowls were cleared away, they tried to think of something cheery to say. But Aunt Jane spoke first.

"I take my hat off to you, Dottie," she said quietly. "It takes courage to make a fresh start like that."

"Thank you, Jane." Dottie dabbed at the corners of her mouth with a napkin. "I soon made new friends in Elmford. And I started The Underground with Martin."

Auntie Two arrived with their dishes of steaming food. Benny piped up, "You didn't run out of fortune cookies yet, did you, Auntie Two?" He sounded worried.

"Not much chance of that," Auntie Two

assured him with a cheery smile. The owner of the Kowloon Restaurant was a middle-aged woman with straight dark hair and sparkling brown eyes. "Like everyone else in town, I'm trying to drum up business, Benny. It just wouldn't do to run out of fortune cookies. Look over there."

Benny followed her gaze to a side table where beige cookies were piled high in a huge blue bowl. His face broke into a big smile. "Oh, there's plenty to go around!" he said.

Violet helped herself to an egg roll, then passed the plate. "Do you make all the fortune cookies yourself, Auntie Two?" she wanted to know.

"Oh, it's certainly a simple enough recipe, Violet. Just eggs and flour, sugar and water. But so many factories churn them out every day, I find it easier to buy them ready-made. Some companies even put lucky numbers on the little slips of paper. My customers seem to enjoy that."

Benny gave the restaurant owner a puzzled frown. There was something else he was wondering about.

Auntie Two caught the look. "What is it, Benny?"

"Is Auntie Two your real name?"

"Benny!" Jessie gave her little brother a warning look. "That's not really any of our business."

Auntie Two laughed. "That's okay, Jessie," she said. Then she turned to the youngest Alden. "The truth is, I'm from a big family, Benny. My nieces and nephews have oodles of aunts. It's hard for the little ones to remember so many names. It makes it easier if they just call us Auntie One, Auntie Two, Auntie Three, and . . . well, it goes all the way up to Auntie Eight!" she told them before she walked away.

Benny kept his eyes fixed on the little beige cookies in the blue bowl. As they finished eating the main courses, he was quick to ask, "Is it time for fortune cookies yet?"

"Not quite, Benny." Martin signaled to Lucy with a wave of his hand. The waitress gave him a smile, then disappeared into the kitchen. "I have a little surprise planned," he said.

A moment later Lucy walked into the dining room carrying a big cake. Martin and Aunt Jane started singing "Happy Birthday," and soon the whole restaurant had joined in. Dottie made a wish and blew out the candles. Then Lucy served chocolate cake to everyone at the table.

"Tonight we get *two* desserts," Benny said, excited. "Cake *and* fortune cookies!"

"That's a dream come true for you, Benny," Henry teased his little brother. Everyone laughed, including Benny.

Aunt Jane turned to Dottie. "I'd love to hear more about your hometown," she said. "What was it like growing up in Keller's Crossing?"

Jessie leaned forward, interested. "Did you run a bookstore there, too?"

For a moment, Dottie said nothing. She just poked at her cake with a fork. When she finally spoke, her voice was strained. "Keller's Crossing was a fine place to grow up," she said. "It will always have a special place in my heart. But the past is best forgotten." Quickly changing the subject, she added, "Now, where are those fortune cookies?"

Jessie stared at Dottie for a moment, wondering why she hadn't answered her question.

Just then, Lucy arrived with one — and *only* one — fortune cookie on a small plate. She went around to the other side of the table and set the plate down in front of Dottie.

Benny looked bewildered. Had Auntie Two run out of fortune cookies after all? No, the blue bowl on the side table was still filled with the bow-shaped cookies. What was going on?

"I'll get more fortune cookies in a minute," Lucy promised, noticing Benny's puzzled frown. "But the birthday girl should open the first one." Then she turned and quickly walked away.

Dottie wasn't having any of this. "You've been waiting long enough, Benny," she said.

She held the plate out to him. "The first one is for you."

Martin put up a hand. "Wait a minute, Dottie. The birthday girl should always open the first — "

Dottie shook her head and cut in with, "Nonsense! The first one's for Benny. And I won't take no for an answer."

"Is it all right, Aunt Jane?" Benny looked over at his aunt expectantly.

Aunt Jane smiled. "Help yourself, Benny."

Benny was grinning from ear to ear. "Thank you very much!" With a few quick motions, he reached for the fortune cookie, broke it in half, and pulled out the fortune.

"Would you like me to read it?" Violet offered. Benny was just learning to read. As Benny passed the fortune to her, she silently read the words on the little slip of paper. Then her eyes widened and she gasped.

CHAPTER 3

The Strange Message

"What is it, Violet?" Jessie asked. "What does it say?" She inched her chair closer to her sister's.

"It's . . . it's the strangest thing," Violet said in a quiet voice. "I've never seen a fortune like *this* before!"

Everyone was staring at Violet in surprise. "Read it, okay?" Benny said, jiggling with excitement.

"All right." Violet nodded. "Here's what it says." Then she read aloud:

"Where rainbows explode,
And tigers twist,
A mystery awaits,
Just choose from the list."

Benny jumped in his chair and clapped his hands. "I knew it! My fortune really *does* say a mystery's coming our way!" His big eyes had grown even rounder.

The others at the table looked at one another. They were too stunned to speak.

Henry reached for the little slip of paper. "It doesn't make any sense," he said after reading it again.

"We'll figure it out," chirped Benny. "We're good detectives."

Violet didn't look so sure. "We've never had a mystery like *this* before."

Jessie giggled. She couldn't help it — it all seemed so funny. "One thing's for sure," she said. "A mystery in a fortune cookie beats everything!"

Everyone laughed — except Martin, who was strangely quiet.

"Hang on a minute!" Henry said as

something caught his eye. "There's a message on the other side of this fortune."

"What does it say?" asked Benny.

"Is it another poem?" Violet questioned at the same time.

Henry read it to them. *"No need to go far."* He looked up. "That's all it says."

"It must be a clue," Benny guessed.

Henry passed the fortune back to his little brother. "Could be."

Martin suddenly spoke up. "I bet it's just somebody's idea of a joke." He sounded annoyed. "What I mean is, a worker in one of those fortune cookie factories was probably just having a bit of fun. That's all."

"I'm not so sure," said Dottie as Lucy arrived with more fortune cookies. "There's something very strange about this."

Hearing the remark, Lucy said, "Is everything all right?"

Martin frowned. "Well, I hope you brought some better fortunes this time. Benny's was a real dud."

"What . . . ?" Lucy's jaw dropped. "What

are you talking about?" She sounded upset.

"I found a mystery in my fortune cookie!" Benny told her, glowing with excitement.

A strange look passed over Lucy's face. As she set the plate of fortune cookies on the table, she almost knocked over Benny's glass of water. Luckily, Violet grabbed it in time and set it back in its place.

Lucy stood twisting her hands. "I . . . I . . . " She shut her mouth.

Jessie glanced at Henry. Why was the waitress so upset? She could tell by the look in Henry's eye that he was wondering the same thing.

Turning to Benny, Lucy said, "I guess there's only one thing to do. You can trade that fortune in for a better one. Would you like that?"

"I wouldn't like that one little bit!" Benny closed his hand over the little slip of paper. "Thanks anyway."

"No, none of us would like that," added Jessie.

Aunt Jane explained, "There's nothing

these children enjoy more than a mystery."

At this, the waitress walked off with a troubled look in her eye.

Jessie turned her attention to the plate of fortune cookies. "I wonder . . . "

"What is it?" Henry asked.

"I was just thinking — maybe we'll find more clues inside the other cookies."

Henry said, "Let's check it out." He reached for a fortune cookie. So did everyone else.

A moment later, Jessie was shaking her head. "No clue in mine," she told them. Then she read aloud: *"Your patience will be rewarded."*

Henry took a look at his fortune. *"Save your money for a rainy day."* He shrugged. "Nothing mysterious about that, either."

It was Violet's turn next. *"Keep an open mind."* She looked on the other side of the little slip of paper. "That's all it says."

Nobody else got any mysterious fortunes, either. Aunt Jane's said, *"Do not rush things this week."* Dottie got, *"Now is the time to move forward."* And Martin's was, *"Actions speak louder than words."* They weren't really sure what kind of clue they were looking for, but they didn't find anything helpful.

"I've never heard of exploding rainbows," said Jessie, taking another look at Benny's fortune.

"Or twisting tigers," put in Violet.

"It's a mystery," said Henry. "That's for sure!"

That night, the four Aldens had a meeting in the bedroom that Jessie and Violet shared. "Who in the world would put such a strange message in a fortune cookie?" Violet asked with a frown.

"And *why?*" demanded Benny.

"We may never know," said Jessie, who was sitting on the bed next to Benny.

"Auntie Two buys her fortune cookies ready-made," Henry reminded them. "Martin might be right. This could be a factory worker's idea of a joke."

Benny shook his head. "My fortune didn't come from a factory."

"How can you be so sure?" asked Violet.

The youngest Alden raced out of the room. When he returned, he was swinging an old sock in the air. He gave the sock a good shake over the bed, and little slips of paper fluttered down. "The fortune I got tonight is different from all the others," he told them.

They all gathered around to take a look at Benny's collection. Sure enough, the other fortunes were all neatly typed in red ink. But the latest fortune had been printed by hand — in *blue* ink.

"You're right, Benny," Jessie said as she compared the fortunes. "That's good detective work," she added, smiling at her little brother.

Benny grinned. "Thanks."

"I just noticed something else." Violet was looking over Jessie's shoulder. "The *i*'s on Benny's fortune are dotted with little hearts." Violet wasn't sure, but she thought it might be some kind of clue.

"Still, we can't be sure a factory worker didn't do it," Henry insisted.

"No, we can't be sure," agreed Jessie.

"But it's also possible someone in Elmford dropped their own fortune cookie into Auntie Two's blue bowl."

Violet agreed. "She keeps the bowl right out in the open—on the side table."

Benny nodded. "Auntie Two said it's simple to make fortune cookies. I bet anybody could do it."

"It did sound easy enough," admitted Henry, backing down a little. "I guess anybody in Elmford could have written that message."

"But . . . who?" Violet wondered.

Henry shrugged. "Beats me!"

"I don't really know, either," said Jessie. "But Lucy *did* seem very nervous tonight. Did you notice?"

"She got our drinks mixed up," Benny recalled. "And she almost spilled my water."

"Lucy just started a new job," Violet was quick to point out. "That's why she was nervous. I don't see anything wrong with that, do you?"

Henry shook his head. "Not if that's all it was."

"Just acting nervous doesn't make her suspicious," Violet insisted. Violet was shy, and being around a lot of people made her nervous, too.

"You're right," Jessie said quietly. "But we have to consider every possibility."

This made sense. But Violet didn't like to be suspicious just because someone was nervous.

"I wonder why Martin was acting so weird," said Henry. "It wasn't like him to get so upset at the bookstore."

"That customer said something about a mysterious disappearance," Benny reminded them in a worried voice. "What did he mean?"

"I don't know," Jessie said. "But I think we should concentrate on one mystery at a time."

Benny grinned. "Let's solve the mystery in the fortune cookie first."

"But where will we find exploding rainbows and twisting tigers?" Jessie wondered.

Violet had an answer. "Near the Kowloon Restaurant," she said. "The fortune said, *No need to go far.*"

"Good thinking, Violet!" said Benny, his grin getting bigger.

Jessie and Henry weren't sure about this. Still, it couldn't hurt to take a look around town in the morning.

CHAPTER 4

Who is Drum Keller?

The Aldens got up early the next morning to surprise Aunt Jane with a special breakfast. They discussed the mystery while they worked.

"I still can't believe it," Jessie was saying as she scrambled eggs in a large bowl. "Imagine finding a mystery in a fortune cookie!"

"I keep wondering where we should look first," said Violet, who was washing strawberries under the tap. "When we get to town, I mean."

Henry looked up. "Unless I miss my guess, the Rainbow's End Jewelry Store might be a good place to start."

The others stared at Henry. Slowly they understood his meaning.

"Oh!" cried Violet. "If a rainbow explodes, then — "

"That's the end of it!" finished Benny.

Henry nodded. "Exactly."

Benny let out a cheer. It was always fun figuring out clues.

"And the jewelry store is right beside The Underground," added Jessie.

Violet nodded. "And that means it's not far from the Kowloon Restaurant."

"Something sure smells good," Aunt Jane said, walking into the kitchen.

"We made breakfast," Jessie told her. "Come and have some."

Aunt Jane pulled up a chair. "You certainly are the early birds today."

"Well, the early bird catches the worm," Henry said with a grin. He set a platter of crispy bacon on the table.

Smiling, Aunt Jane said, "I have a hunch

you won't be looking for worms today."

"You're right, Aunt Jane." Benny's eyes were shining. "We'll be looking for clues!"

"We thought we'd ride into town after breakfast," Jessie said as she dished up the scrambled eggs.

"If you don't mind, Aunt Jane," Violet was quick to add.

Aunt Jane didn't mind at all. She knew the Aldens were never happier than when they were tracking clues. "Just beware of exploding rainbows and twisting tigers!" she said. She sounded serious, but there was a teasing twinkle in her eye.

After breakfast, when the dishes had been washed and put away, the Aldens set off on the bikes their aunt kept for them. As they pedaled along the dirt roads, Violet looked over at Jessie, who was riding beside her.

"Don't you just love the sweet country air?" she asked.

Jessie took a deep breath and nodded. "I can smell dried grass and wildflowers."

When the Aldens arrived in town, they put their bikes in a bike rack. Then they walked the short distance from the parking lot to Elmford's Main Street. The children had visited Aunt Jane so many times, they knew their way around the little town very well.

Henry's gaze took in the tidy little shops that lined both sides of the street. "Let's check out the Rainbow's End Jewelry Store."

"Rainbows can't really explode," said Benny as he fell into step beside Henry. Then he frowned a little. "Can they?"

Henry shook his head. "I've never heard of it."

"Rainbows just fade away," said Violet.

Benny was still busy thinking. "And there's no such thing as twisting tigers, right?"

"Right," said Jessie. "Somebody just has a good imagination."

Violet had a thought. "Maybe the jewelry store has a brooch or a necklace with a twisting tiger or a colorful rainbow on it."

"Could be," said Henry.

As the Aldens neared the jewelry store, a

voice behind them said, "Well, look who's here!"

The children turned around and saw Dottie coming up the stone steps from The Underground. She looked at the Aldens curiously. "What brings you into town again so soon?"

Benny ran over to her, bursting with news. "We'll be solving the fortune cookie mystery in no time, Dottie!" he said. "Henry figured out one of the clues already."

Raising her eyebrows, Dottie said, "Well, imagine that!" She seemed delighted.

"We're not really sure we're on the right track," Henry was quick to add. "But we think Benny's fortune might be leading us to the Rainbow's End Jewelry Store."

"Would you mind if I tag along?" Dottie asked. "Maybe I can sniff out a clue or two."

"We'd love to have you join us," Violet told her, speaking for them all.

As they stepped inside the jewelry store, Benny suddenly spotted another familiar face. Martin Howard was staring through the glass countertop at the sparkling array of rings and watches. He seemed to be lost in thought.

"Hi, Martin!" Benny called out to him.

Suddenly, Martin jerked his head around. "Oh!" He looked startled to see the Aldens. Then he caught sight of his business partner and his face turned bright red.

Dottie gave him a puzzled smile. "What are *you* doing here, Martin?"

The question seemed to catch him off guard. "What . . . ?"

"I didn't know you took an interest in jewelry."

"I . . . I was just looking at, um . . . watches," Martin stammered.

"Watches?" echoed Dottie. "But . . . you already have *two* beautiful watches, Martin."

"A person can have *three* watches, can't he?" Martin cut in a little gruffly.

Jessie looked at Henry, but she didn't say anything. She thought Martin seemed very nervous.

Just then, a woman in a blue business suit

came out from the back room. She was carrying a tiny velvet box in her hand. "You're going to love this, Martin," she said. "It's the most stunning—"

Martin held up a hand. "No! No, I don't want to see it right now!" His voice sounded tense. "I don't have time to stand around looking at watches all day."

The salesclerk gave Martin a peculiar look. "Watches? But I thought — "

Martin's forehead was beading with perspiration. "I, uh, I have to leave. Right now. I just remembered that I forgot something." With that, he turned on his heel and rushed out.

The woman behind the counter let out a sigh. "For the life of me, I'll never understand people!" Then she disappeared into the back again.

"What was that all about?" Henry wondered aloud.

Violet added, "Martin's usually so friendly."

"Always such a perfect gentleman," Dottie agreed. "Goodness, he was acting as though he'd just been caught doing something wrong."

Soon they forgot all about Martin as they set to work searching for exploding rainbows and twisting tigers. They looked carefully at all the displays of lockets and necklaces, brooches and bracelets, watches and rings, tie clips and earrings. But they found nothing that would help with the mystery.

Outside, Henry said, "I guess we weren't on the right track after all."

"Now what?" said Benny.

"Why not check out the other stores on Main Street?" Dottie suggested. Then, with a cheery wave, she dashed back to The Underground.

Nobody had any better ideas, so the Aldens continued down Main Street. "Anything unusual can be a clue," Henry reminded them, "or an answer to a clue."

They kept their eyes open, but there were no exploding rainbows or twisting tigers in any of the stores along the way. After a while, Benny stopped to watch a man wearing a red rubber nose. The man was in front of Albert's Fruit and Vegetable Cellar handing out balloons to the customers.

Benny turned to Henry. "That clown's handing out balloons."

"That's true," Henry said, giving his brother a puzzled look.

"And the balloons are in every color of the rainbow!"

"Wait a minute!" said Henry. "You might be onto something, Benny. Balloons explode if you prick them with a pin."

"Do you think the clues are leading us *here*?" Jessie asked in disbelief. "To Albert's Fruit and Vegetable Cellar?"

"Anything's possible," said Henry. "Clowns are in the circus, and so are lions and tigers."

"Let's take a look around," Violet suggested.

The Aldens searched through the shop once . . . twice . . . three times. They found oranges and apples, bananas and plums, turnips and potatoes, carrots and celery, onions and cabbages. But no clues.

When they stepped outside, the man in the red rubber nose offered Benny a balloon. But Benny just shook his head. "Thanks anyway," he said. Then he walked away with his shoulders slumped.

"Never mind," Jessie said, ruffling her little brother's hair. "It was worth a shot."

As they continued along the sidewalk, Violet suddenly spun around to face her sister and brothers. "I just thought of something! We need to go back."

"Back?" echoed Henry. "You mean the way we came?"

Violet nodded. "Maybe Benny's on the right track about the circus."

"But, Violet," said Jessie, "Elmford doesn't have a circus."

"There's another name for it," Violet told them. "For the circus, I mean."

Henry, Jessie, and Benny stared at her. They looked totally confused. Then Jessie snapped her fingers in sudden understand-

ing. "Some people call the circus the *big top*!"

Benny scrunched up his face. "I don't get it."

"I think I do," said Henry. "You're talking about the Big Top T-Shirt Shop, aren't you, Violet?"

With that, the children hurried back along Main Street. Inside the T-shirt shop, Benny made a beeline straight for the salesman. "Excuse me, please," he said. "I was wondering if you have any shirts with exploding rainbows or twisting tigers on them."

His brother and sisters exchanged smiles. They could always count on Benny not to waste time on small talk.

The salesman rolled his eyes. "Look, I just started this job today," he said irritably. "I have no idea what's here." Then he turned his back on Benny and walked away.

Benny spoke in a small voice. "I tried to be polite."

"You *were* polite, Benny." Violet stepped up beside her brother and put a comforting arm around him.

"We can look through the T-shirts ourselves. It won't take long if we split up," Jessie suggested in her practical way.

Jessie and Violet set to work checking out the T-shirts on the shelves. Henry and Benny searched through the T-shirts piled on the half-price table. They looked and looked. But they didn't find any T-shirts with exploding rainbows or twisting tigers on them.

At last, they stepped outside. "Looks like we struck out again," Violet admitted.

Henry shook his head. "It's a real mess in there," he remarked. "No wonder that new salesman didn't know what T-shirts they had."

"What now?" Benny wanted to know.

Henry looked at his wristwatch. "Why don't we figure it out over lunch?"

"Great idea!" cried Benny. He gave his brother the thumbs-up sign.

Soon they were all settled in a booth at the Elmford Coffee Shop. "Maybe we didn't find any clues," Violet said. "But at least we didn't come away empty-handed." She held up a shopping bag.

Jessie smiled. "Won't Grandfather be surprised?"

"I can't wait for him to see it," added Benny.

As Henry passed out the menus, he said, "What could be a better gift for Grandfather than a T-shirt with 'World's Greatest Grandfather' on it?"

When the waitress arrived, Henry ordered a toasted cheese sandwich and a cola. Jessie had a chicken sandwich, cole slaw, and milk. Violet chose tuna on a bun and lemonade. And Benny ordered a hamburger, fries, and chocolate milk. The waitress wrote down their orders and hurried away.

While they waited for their food, the Aldens turned their attention back to the mystery. "Isn't it funny?" Jessie remarked. "The clues seemed to fit so many places."

Nodding, Henry started adding everything up on his fingers. "First, there was the Rainbow's End Jewelry Store, then Albert's Fruit and Vegetable Cellar, and finally the Big Top T-Shirt Shop."

"That seems weird," said Violet.

Henry shrugged. "It's amazing what you can talk yourself into."

"What do you mean, Henry?" Benny wanted to know.

"Well . . . " Henry hesitated. "It turns out the clues weren't really leading us to any of those places," he pointed out. "Maybe we just made the clues fit because . . . " He paused for a moment to sort out his thoughts. "Well, because we wanted to believe there was a real mystery to solve."

The corners of Benny's mouth turned down. "You mean this isn't a real mystery?" He looked crushed.

There was a long silence. In a quiet voice, Henry finally answered Benny's question. "It's beginning to look that way."

Violet bit her lip. "I really don't know what to believe."

"I don't, either," put in Jessie. "But I guess it's possible we got all worked up about nothing. Maybe Martin was right after all. Maybe the fortune was just some prank."

Benny didn't look very happy to hear that. The enthusiasm seemed to drain out of him.

No one said anything for a while. There was nothing to say. If the fortune was just a prank, then there wasn't a mystery to solve.

As the waitress brought their food, Benny spoke up. "We can't just do *nothing*, can we?" he protested.

Violet felt her brother's disappointment. "Maybe we should check out a few more stores."

"Okay, Benny," Henry said. "We'll go to *all* the stores."

"We promise," added Jessie.

Benny felt more cheerful after hearing this. "Maybe we can check out the ice cream parlor next," Benny suggested, with a grin on his face. He dipped a french fry into ketchup. "And while we're there, we can get — "

"Ice-cream cones for dessert!" finished Violet, who couldn't help laughing.

Jessie swallowed a bite of her sandwich. "Are you sure you'll have room for dessert, Benny, after a hamburger and so many fries?" She smiled as she waited for her younger brother's answer, even though she knew what it would be.

"I *always* have room for ice cream!" said Benny, who loved desserts. He turned to his brother. "Do we have enough money for ice cream, Henry?"

But Henry didn't seem to hear Benny. He had spotted someone sitting at a nearby booth. It was Martin! He was sipping coffee and talking on a cell phone.

"Of course I'm not getting cold feet!" Martin said into the phone, sounding annoyed. "I'm telling you, there was nothing I could do. It all happened too fast."

Henry put his finger to his lips. "Don't look now," he whispered to the others, "but Martin is here."

One by one, the other Aldens peeked over to take a look. "You're right, Henry," Jessie said, trying not to stare.

Violet turned around slowly to take another glance. "I wonder why he looks upset," she said in a hushed voice.

The children didn't mean to eavesdrop. But from where they were sitting, they couldn't help overhearing bits and pieces of the phone conversation.

"Don't forget, you're dealing with Drum Keller." Martin was talking loudly now. "Even a hint of something fishy going on and it'll ruin everything!"

Jessie held a forkful of coleslaw in midair. "Did . . . did he just say something fishy was going on?"

"Yes," Henry answered. None of them liked the sound of this.

Just then, Martin pocketed his cell phone, got to his feet, and walked out of the coffee shop. As the door closed, the Aldens leaned closer together and began speaking in low voices.

"Do you think something fishy really *is* going on?" Violet said in alarm.

"I hope not." Jessie found it difficult to swallow. She put down her fork. "I really

like Martin. He's always been so nice to us."
She didn't like to think of him doing anything wrong.

Henry took a sip of his cola. "He was acting weird in the jewelry store today."

Jessie nodded. "He looked as if we'd
caught him in the middle of something he
wanted to keep secret."

The four children fell silent for a while.
They were all wondering the same things.
Who was Drum Keller? And what on earth
was Martin Howard up to?

CHAPTER 5

Fortune Cookie Delight

The afternoon was getting hot as the Aldens headed for the Elmford Ice Cream Parlor. When they stepped inside, Benny stopped in his tracks. "Isn't that Lucy, from the Kowloon Restaurant?"

"I'm sure of it," said Violet, glancing over at the young woman standing at the counter. Although Lucy's back was turned to them, Violet recognized the waitress's thick auburn hair, pulled back with a green headband. Lucy was deep in conversation with Angela, the owner of the Elmford Ice Cream Parlor.

Angela was standing behind the counter, shaking her head. "I just can't get over it!" she said. "A secret identity! It's so exciting."

"The whole thing makes me nervous," responded Lucy. "What if something else goes wrong?"

"Did you hear that?" Violet whispered as Jessie and Henry came up behind them.

Jessie nodded. "I wonder what Angela meant about a secret identity."

Just then, Benny stepped up to the counter. "Hi, Lucy. Remember us?"

"Oh!" Noticing the children for the first time, Lucy seemed startled. But she pulled herself together quickly. "Yes, of course I do. You're the Aldens," she said, smiling uneasily. "I was . . . uh, just checking out the ice cream flavors." She seemed unable to look them in the eye. "Anyway, I think I'll go find a quiet table and read for a while." She quickly walked away, leaving the Aldens to stare after her.

"That was pretty strange, wasn't it?" remarked Violet.

Benny sighed. "I don't think anyone in town likes us."

"I'm sure they like us just fine, Benny," Jessie assured him. But she couldn't help thinking that people in Elmsford suddenly seemed very eager to get away from them. First Martin. Then Lucy. It was hard to figure out what was happening in the little town.

Angela spoke up. "What'll it be today, kids?"

"Ice-cream cones, please!" Benny told her. "But we haven't decided what kind we want."

"Take your time." Angela smiled at the youngest Alden. "I'm not going anywhere."

The children turned their attention to the metal containers of ice cream that were lined up in the freezer under the glass countertop. There were so many flavors, it was hard to choose.

"That Strawberry Swirl looks good," said Violet.

"I think I'll get it," Jessie said. "What are you having?"

After much thought, Violet decided on Blueberry Joy.

"I might give the Peanut Butter Crunch a try," put in Henry. Then he turned to his little brother. "Benny, do you know what you want?"

"I can't decide between the Chocolate Chip and the — " Benny suddenly stopped talking. He froze on the spot.

"What is it, Benny?" Violet wanted to know.

Benny swiveled around on his heel. "It's ice cream!" he almost shouted.

Henry's eyebrows furrowed. "Of course it's ice cream, Benny," he said in a puzzled tone. "This is an ice cream parlor, remember?"

Jessie could tell by her little brother's face that he had discovered something important. "What's going on, Benny?" she asked, stepping up beside him.

"Look!" Benny pointed through the glass countertop. "The ice cream in that bucket is speckled with every color of the rainbow! And look at the one next to it," he added, hopping up and down on one foot. "It's striped just like a tiger!" The others huddled closer to look down at the containers of ice cream.

"Omigosh!" Violet blinked. "I can't believe it."

Henry shook his head in amazement as he stared at the bucket of colorfully speckled ice cream labeled: RAINBOW EXPLOSION. Beside it was a bucket of orange-and-black striped ice cream called: TIGER'S TWIST. "Way to go, Benny!" Henry smiled at his little brother.

"See?" Benny said. "The mystery in the fortune cookie wasn't just a joke." He put his hand up and each Alden gave him a high five.

Jessie began to recite the words on Benny's fortune, and the others soon joined in. *"Where rainbows explode,/ And tigers twist,/ A mystery awaits,/ Just choose from the list."* They all knew the poem by heart. "But where is the list?" Jessie wondered.

Violet spotted a list of ice cream flavors on the wall by the door. "That's got to be it!"

"It's the only list around," agreed Henry. They went over to take a closer look.

Jessie read off the ice cream flavors. There was everything from Cherries Jubilee to Peach Crumble. When she got to the end of the list, she suddenly clapped her hands. "Look, they have a Mystery Flavor of the Week!"

"*A mystery awaits,/ Just choose from the list!*" repeated Violet in a hushed voice.

"That's what I'm going to choose," Benny decided. "The Mystery Flavor of the Week."

The Aldens hurried back to the counter and placed their order — Strawberry Swirl for Jessie, Blueberry Joy for Violet, Peanut Butter Crunch for Henry, and the Mystery Flavor of the Week for Benny.

Angela looked pleased. "So you're willing to try my latest invention, are you, Benny?"

"You *invented* the mystery flavor?" Benny's eyes were wide with interest.

"Of course. All my ice cream is home-made, you know." Lowering her voice, Angela added, "The mystery flavor this week is Fortune Cookie Delight."

The Aldens could hardly believe their ears. "Fortune Cookie Delight?" echoed Benny.

Angela nodded. "It's made with caramel ice cream — and there's a fortune cookie on the very top." She paused as she pushed back a loose strand of hair. "Do you think it's a good idea?" She looked hopefully at the Aldens.

"Is it a real fortune cookie?" Benny wanted to know.

"You bet!"

"With a real fortune inside?"

"For sure." Angela smiled at the youngest Alden.

"Then it's a great idea!" Benny concluded. And the others agreed.

"Whew!" Angela seemed relieved to hear this. "I'm hoping my latest mystery flavor will do the trick. Drum up business, I mean."

"I'm sure it will!" said a cheery voice behind the Aldens. They turned around to see

Martin walking over with Dottie by his side.

Jessie caught Henry's eye. Martin had sounded so grumpy on the phone just a short time ago. Was it possible that his cheerfulness was just an act?

"All the local store owners are doing a terrific job," Martin went on. "Bringing shoppers into town, I mean. And it's not easy these days."

Dottie nodded as she looked around at the empty tables. "That new shopping center on the highway really draws the crowds away from downtown. But we're all doing our best to bring the customers back. Right, Angela?"

"That's for sure," she said. "Mr. Albert even hired a clown."

"Entertainment and a free balloon for the kids." Martin nodded his head approvingly. "Terrific sales gimmick."

"Sales gimmick?" Benny made a face.

Henry smiled over at his little brother. "A sales gimmick's an idea for attracting customers, Benny."

"That's exactly right," agreed Martin. "All the store owners are trying to come up with something."

Angela was busy scooping ice cream into cones. "I suppose you'll be having your usual flavor, Dottie."

"You guessed it!"

"Every week we come in here at this time," Martin told the Aldens, "and every week my partner chooses the Mystery Flavor."

"I can never resist a good mystery!" Dottie said. "By the way," she added, looking at the Aldens, "how's it going with that mystery of *yours*?"

Henry said only, "We're still working on it." He didn't want to talk about it in front of Martin.

"Well, let me know what happens," said Dottie. "I'm fascinated." Spotting Lucy, she hurried away to say hello, with Martin right behind her.

Benny's eyes widened in excitement as Angela handed him his cone with the fortune cookie on top. The Aldens paid for

their ice cream and sat down at a small table by the window. Benny wasted no time removing the cookie, breaking it open, and pulling out the little white slip of paper.

"Will you read it, Jessie?" he said, handing her the fortune.

Jessie studied it for a moment, then she frowned.

"Is it a clue?" Benny asked her.

"I'm not sure," she said.

"Don't keep us in the dark, Jessie," Henry pleaded. "What does it say?"

Jessie tucked her hair behind her ears and read aloud:

> "*Twenty-four plus two,*
> *Will give you a clue.*"

Benny crinkled his brow. "What does *that* mean?"

Jessie shrugged. Benny looked at Henry and then at Violet. They didn't seem to have any answers, either.

"Do the *i*'s have little hearts over them?"

Violet couldn't help asking. "Like the last fortune, I mean."

Jessie nodded. "*And* it's neatly printed by hand in blue ink."

Violet felt a shiver go up her spine. This was getting more and more mysterious.

"Is there a message on the other side?" Henry wanted to know.

Jessie hadn't thought of that. She turned the fortune over. Instead of a message, there were numbers grouped together. Jessie read them aloud:

"6-9-14-4 4-18-21-13 11-5-12-12-5-18
9-14 20-8-5 3-5-12-12-1-18."

"Wow!" Benny was so interested in the latest fortune, he had forgotten all about his ice-cream cone. "I bet it's a secret code!" he said, his voice rising in excitement.

Jessie looked around and realized that Martin and Lucy were staring at them. "We can't really talk here," she said quietly.

Henry nodded. "Let's go."

Dottie suddenly called out to the children. "Nothing mysterious in *my* fortune cookie." She was sitting at a corner table with Martin and Lucy. "How about yours?"

The Aldens all looked at each other, not sure what to say. "A bunch of numbers," Jessie said at last.

Dottie nodded. "*Lucky* numbers, no doubt." She looked disappointed.

On their way out, Jessie stopped at the counter. "I was just wondering, Angela," she said. "Where do you get your fortune cookies?"

Angela waved the question off. "Oh, most grocery stores carry them. Anybody can buy boxes of fortune cookies. Why do you ask, Jessie?"

"Oh, no reason," Jessie said with a shrug. When she turned around, she noticed that Martin was watching them closely, his eyes narrowed.

"Do you think Dottie's right?" Benny asked as they went outside. "About lucky numbers, I mean."

"No," Henry said firmly. "I think *you're* right, Benny. It's definitely some kind of code."

As they finished their ice cream and walked to their bikes, Jessie looked back over her shoulder. She couldn't shake the feeling that they were being watched. Was it just her imagination, or was somebody following them?

"What is it, Jessie?" Henry asked. He could see that something was troubling her.

"Nothing really," said Jessie, keeping her voice low. She didn't want to frighten Violet and Benny, who were walking ahead. "I just feel like we're being watched."

Henry stopped in the middle of the sidewalk and looked behind him. "I don't see anyone."

Jessie looked back down the street also. She saw only shoppers coming and going, the same as always. Licking a drop of strawberry ice cream from the back of her hand, she said, "It's probably nothing." But there was a small part of her that didn't believe it for a minute.

CHAPTER 6

A Clue in the Soup

The Aldens puzzled and puzzled over the strange coded message. But the next afternoon, they were still stumped. None of them had seen a code like this before. Even Aunt Jane, who had been eager to see the latest fortune, couldn't come up with any answers.

"How are we going to figure out this clue?" said Violet. She turned down the heat under the alphabet soup. The four children were busy making lunch. While they worked, they discussed the case.

"Why don't we go over what we know about the mystery," suggested Henry, who was squeezing lemons to make lemonade.

"Which one?" Benny set the soup bowls on the table. "The mystery we found inside the fortune cookie? Or the mystery of who put it there and why?"

"And don't forget the third mystery," Henry added. "*Somebody* has a secret identity!"

Jessie was buttering the bread for sandwiches. "At least that's what Angela and Lucy think."

Benny suddenly frowned. "But . . . what exactly is a secret identity?"

Henry added water and sugar to the lemon juice. "It means there's more to somebody than meets the eye," he told his brother. "A person with a secret identity sometimes goes by another name. An alias." He stirred the lemonade with a big wooden spoon.

"Do you think that somebody in Elmford has a secret identity?" Jessie wondered.

"Could be," said Violet. "Martin was

talking on the phone about something fishy going on, remember?"

"And he mentioned somebody named Drum Keller," Henry recalled. He thought about this for a minute, then he got out Aunt Jane's phone book and began thumbing through the white pages. Finally, he turned to the others. "Just as I suspected. There's no listing in Elmford for Drum Keller."

Jessie raised an eyebrow. "Are you sure?" she said, walking over.

"It ought to be right here." Henry had the phone book opened on the counter. He placed his finger halfway down the page.

"Drum Keller might be new in town," offered Violet. "Maybe his or her phone isn't connected yet. Or maybe Drum Keller is just a nickname."

"Maybe," said Henry. But he didn't sound as if he believed it. "Or . . . maybe somebody in town used to go by that name but doesn't anymore."

"You think Drum Keller is somebody's secret identity?" Benny's eyes were huge.

"Could be," said Henry.

Violet looked over at Henry as she stirred the soup. "Why would someone in Elmford need a secret identity?"

Putting the phone book away, Henry shrugged a little. "I have no idea," he answered. "Maybe there's somebody here who wants to hide something from his past."

Benny placed the soup bowls on the table. "Dottie didn't want to talk about *her* past," he reminded them. "Remember?"

"Oh, Benny!" cried Violet. "You don't really think Dottie has a secret identity, do you?"

Benny thought a bit. "Well, she didn't want to talk about her hometown," he argued. "She said the past was best forgotten."

"That's because it made her sad to think about her husband," put in Violet. "That's all it was."

Jessie frowned as she brought over the egg salad sandwiches. She thought there was more to it than that. But she didn't say anything.

"I still wonder what the man in the bookstore meant," said Henry. "About a mysterious disappearance, I mean." He poured lemonade into Benny's pink cup. Benny had found the cracked pink cup when they were living in the boxcar. He always brought it with him when they traveled.

"Just one mystery at a time, remember?" Violet said as they sat down at the table. "If we put our heads together, maybe we can figure out the fortune cookie mystery." And the others agreed.

Benny helped himself to a sandwich. "One thing's for sure, somebody in Elmford knows we're detectives."

"What makes you say that, Benny?" Violet wanted to know.

"Well, why else would we keep getting those mysterious fortunes?" he said.

"We can't be certain, Benny," said Henry. "But it does seem like those fortunes were meant just for us."

Jessie agreed. "Nobody else seems to be getting any weird messages — and we got *two*."

"That means Angela's fortune cookies didn't come from the grocery store," Benny pointed out. "I wonder why she lied to us."

Jessie thought about this. "Angela didn't actually say that's where *she* got them, Benny."

Benny looked confused.

"When I asked about the fortune cookies," Jessie went on, "Angela said anybody can buy them at the grocery store."

"You're right, Jessie," Violet realized. "She didn't actually say that's where *she* got *hers*." She swallowed a spoonful of alphabet soup. "Maybe Angela and Auntie Two put the weird messages in the fortune cookies."

The others had to admit it was possible. After all, Angela had invented Fortune Cookie Delight as the Mystery Flavor of the Week. And weren't Angela and Auntie Two both trying to drum up business? What could be a better sales gimmick than hiding clues inside fortune cookies?

"I still think our best suspect is Lucy," Benny insisted. He drained the last of his lemonade. "We never got any weird fortunes at the Kowloon Restaurant until she started working for Auntie Two."

"It *was* kind of funny that she was at the ice cream parlor," Henry said after a moment's thought, "just when Benny got another strange fortune."

"Dottie was there, too." Jessie poured more lemonade. "And she seems to be taking quite an interest in the mystery."

Benny nodded. "She wanted to sniff out clues."

"We're forgetting a suspect," Violet said. "Martin."

Henry put down his soup spoon. "Martin's up to something, all right. I'm just not sure it has anything to do with the fortune cookie mystery."

"Unless . . . " Violet began and then stopped herself.

"Are you wondering if the whole town is in on this?" Jessie asked. Then she quickly added, "I don't blame you, Violet. I've wondered about that myself."

"Perhaps we shouldn't mention the mystery to anyone," Violet suggested. "I think we should figure out a few things on our own first."

Henry nodded. "And we'll keep a close eye on all of them — Martin, Dottie, Lucy, Angela, and Auntie Two."

"If only we could figure out what the numbers mean." Benny took a bite of his sandwich while he thought about it. Then he pulled the fortune from his shirt pocket. "*Twenty-four plus two,/ Will give you a clue*," he mumbled because his mouth was full. "Twenty-four plus two makes twenty-six." He scratched his head. "The number twenty-six isn't much to go on."

Henry stared at Benny. A funny look came over his face.

"Is anything wrong, Henry?" asked Jessie.

Henry didn't answer. As he looked down at his bowl of steaming soup, an idea began to form in his mind. Then he slapped his forehead with the palm of his hand. "Of course!" he suddenly said, more to himself than anyone else. "We should have known."

"Henry?" Jessie asked. "Tell us what you're thinking."

Henry was smiling. "The answer to the code is right here!" he told them. He sounded excited.

"Where?" Benny sat up straighter and stopped eating.

"Right here in this bowl," answered Henry, stirring the soup a little with his spoon. The alphabet noodles swirled around and around.

The others stared at Henry. They looked totally confused. What on earth did alphabet soup have to do with the mysterious code?

"When Benny mentioned the number twenty-six," said Henry, "something just clicked. That's exactly how many letters are in the alphabet!" Henry paused to look at his brother and sisters, hoping they would understand what he was driving at. Seeing their puzzled expressions, he explained, "It suddenly hit me, what if each number stands for a different letter in the alphabet?"

Henry stood up and went to get a piece of paper and a pencil. When he sat down again, he printed the alphabet. Then under each letter, he carefully printed a number.

A B C D E F G H I J K L M N
1 2 3 4 5 6 7 8 9 10 11 12 13 14

O P Q R S T U V W X Y Z
15 16 17 18 19 20 21 22 23 24 25 26

Violet gasped. "Oh, I see what you mean!"

"We can match the letters with the numbers in the code!" Jessie added, catching on at the same time.

No one dared breathe as Henry matched up the letters with the numbers.

6-9-14-4   4-18-21-13   11-5-12-12-5-18
F-I-N-D   D-R-U-M   K-E-L-L-E-R
9-14   20-8-5   3-5-12-12-1-18
I-N   T-H-E   C-E-L-L-A-R

Who in the world was Drum Keller? And what was he doing in a cellar?

CHAPTER 7

In the Cellar

"This fortune cookie mystery is getting weirder and weirder," Violet said as they cleared the table after lunch.

"I'll tell you what's weird," Benny said, putting the placemats away. "That name! Drum Keller, I mean."

Jessie filled the sink with warm, soapy water. "I was thinking that, too," she said. There was something oddly familiar about the name Drum Keller, but Jessie couldn't quite put her finger on what it was. She tucked the thought in the back of her mind for the time being.

"So, what's next?" Violet reached for a dish towel.

Henry was ready with an answer. "If you ask me, we should take another bike ride into town." He stacked the soup bowls on the counter. "It's time to find Drum Keller in — "

"The cellar," said Jessie, finishing her older brother's sentence. "The problem is, we don't have a clue what cellar he's in."

"And why on earth is he *in* a cellar?" put in Violet. "What's that all about?"

"It's a mystery," said Henry. "That's for sure."

"We can handle it," Benny insisted. As he dried his pink cup, he had a thought. "Maybe we should look in Albert's Fruit and Vegetable Cellar!"

"Good idea, Benny!" Henry said as he wiped the counters. "Drum Keller *would* make a great name for a clown."

"Yeah," said Benny, getting excited.

"*And* that would explain why he's in a

cellar!" added Violet, who sounded just as excited as Benny.

After putting away the dishes and writing a note for Aunt Jane, the Aldens hopped on their bikes and pedaled as fast as they could into Elmford. Parking their bikes in the lot again, they quickly made their way to Albert's Fruit and Vegetable Cellar.

Benny walked up to the man in the red rubber nose. "Excuse me." He tugged on the clown's polka-dotted sleeve. "Are you Drum Keller?"

"No, sirree!" The man handing out balloons shook his head. "You're looking at the one and only Buttons the Clown."

Benny was disappointed, but he wasn't giving up so easily. He hurried over to the store owner, who was standing near the counter. "Excuse me, Mr. Albert," Benny said. "I was wondering if there's a Drum Keller around here."

"A Drum Keller?" Mr. Albert was polishing an apple. He blinked in surprise. "What's that?" he wanted to know. "Some new kind of onion?"

Benny sighed heavily. "No, Drum Keller's not an onion. At least, I don't think so. Thanks anyway."

As they walked away, Henry said, "Well, I guess that rules out Albert's Fruit and Vegetable Cellar."

Halfway down the block, Jessie suddenly directed their attention to a sign in the window of Wiggins Department Store. "Look. There's a two-for-one sale!"

"But, Jessie," said Violet, sounding puzzled, "we didn't bring money to buy any — "

Jessie broke in before Violet could finish. "The two-for-one sale is in Wiggins' bargain *basement*!"

"And a basement is just like a *cellar*!" Henry was impressed. "Good thinking, Jessie."

Benny's frown disappeared. "Maybe *this* is where Drum Keller works!" he said, holding the door open for the others. "Let's find out."

"Yes, let's," Jessie agreed, quickening her step.

Downstairs, a smiling young woman

asked them, "Are you looking for anything in particular?"

"We sure are," Benny answered. "We're looking for Drum Keller."

"Drum Keller?" The young saleswoman looked puzzled. "Is that a new line of designer jeans?"

Violet had to bite her lip to keep from laughing. "No, we're not looking for jeans," she explained. "Drum Keller's a person."

Jessie added, "At least, that's what we think."

"Does anyone by that name work here?" Henry asked.

The salesclerk shook her head. "I'm afraid not."

On the way out, Violet said, "How do you like that! First, Mr. Albert thinks Drum Keller's an onion. Then the saleswoman thinks Drum Keller's a new line of designer jeans." She paused. "Maybe Drum Keller *isn't* a person. Maybe Drum Keller's a *thing*."

"Maybe." Benny sighed. "I wonder if we'll ever get to the bottom of this."

"I'm sure we will." Jessie sounded positive. Inside, though, she wasn't sure they'd ever find Drum Keller.

Violet noticed that Henry had been very quiet. "Thinking about something, Henry?" she asked.

"What?" Henry had been deep in his own thoughts. "Oh, it's just that something occurred to me," he said slowly. "A cellar's under the ground. Right?"

The others nodded. "Right."

"Well — " Henry began to say, but Jessie interrupted.

"The Underground Bookstore!" she cried. "That's what you're thinking, isn't it, Henry?"

Henry nodded. "It's worth checking out."

Inside the bookstore, they found Dottie sorting through a pile of dusty old books.

"Hi, kids!" She smiled over at them. Then she pointed to the framed photograph hanging on the wall. "Thanks again for such a wonderful gift," she said. "By the way, are you still on the case?"

Benny nodded. "We figured out the — "

Henry poked him. Then Benny remembered they were not supposed to tell anyone about the mystery.

Dottie was instantly curious. "You figured out a clue?"

The children looked at one another. They didn't want to lie, but they also knew it was best not to discuss the mystery just yet. Not until they'd figured a few things out on their own.

Henry quickly changed the subject. "Does anyone else work here, Dottie? Besides you and Martin, I mean."

"Somebody by the name of Drum Keller," Benny added.

Dottie's smile faded. "What . . . ?" She gave the children a sharp look. "Nobody else works here," she said quickly. Then she turned her back, clearly not wanting to talk anymore.

Jessie and Henry exchanged glances. They were pretty sure that Dottie was covering something up.

After leading the others out of earshot, Henry suggested looking around for clues.

So the Aldens split up and began to wander up and down the aisles, keeping their eyes peeled for anything unusual.

After a few minutes of looking, Jessie walked over to her sister and said, "I haven't found anything but books, have you, Violet?"

Violet didn't answer. Her jaw had suddenly dropped.

"What is it, Violet?" asked Jessie.

"It . . . it's Drum Keller!" Violet almost yelled, but stopped herself just in time.

Henry came rushing over. Benny was close behind.

"What's going on?" asked Henry.

Violet was staring through the glass doors of a cabinet filled with old books. She turned halfway around and looked at the others. "It's a mystery series," she told them, her eyes huge. "And you won't believe who wrote them!"

Jessie stepped closer and peered through the glass doors. "Oh!" She put one hand over her mouth in surprise. "Drum Keller!"

Violet nodded. "And the name of the se-

ries is — The Fortune Cookie Mysteries!"

Astounded, the Aldens stood staring at the books for a moment. Then Benny said, "So Drum Keller is an author?"

Henry nodded. "Looks that way, Benny." He thought for a moment. Then he said, "Remember the other night before dinner, when Martin got so mad at that customer?" The others nodded. "Weren't the books in this case the ones Dottie was refusing to sell?"

"Yes," Jessie said. Then she added, "She said she wouldn't sell them for *any* price."

"I wonder why," said Violet.

Just then, Benny spotted something out of the corner of his eye. He looked closer and blinked in disbelief. "Is . . . is that what I think it is?" he asked.

The others looked to where Benny was pointing. In a dark corner of one of the cabinet shelves was a fortune cookie!

"Do you think it's part of the display?" Jessie wondered.

"Maybe," said Henry. "But I doubt it. After all, the clues led us right here." Henry opened the glass door. Reaching inside, he pulled out the little bow-shaped cookie.

"What does the fortune say?" Benny's voice was high with excitement.

"Let's look at it later," Henry said, barely moving his lips. "Right now, just act casual. We're being watched."

Sure enough, Dottie was giving them a sideways glance.

"I think it's time to go," Jessie remarked, and no one argued.

"Thanks for letting us look around, Dottie," said Violet as the Aldens waved goodbye and quickly walked to the door. Just outside, the four children stopped in their tracks at the sound of a familiar voice.

"No, no, no!" Martin was standing at the top of the stone steps that led up from The Underground. He sounded upset. "I don't want her to have anything more to do with this business. She's ruining everything."

"I know things haven't been working out the way you wanted." This was Auntie Two speaking. She was standing with her back to the children.

"You can say that again!" interrupted Martin. "I can't risk any more mix-ups."

From where they were standing in the stairwell, the children could see Martin hand Auntie Two a small envelope.

"I'm counting on your help," said Martin.

"Don't worry," said Auntie Two. She dropped the envelope into her purse without opening it. "Soon Howard will be the only name on the door to The Underground." Auntie Two and Martin stepped out of sight, their voices fading away.

Henry crept up the steps and looked around. When he gestured that the coast was clear, the others followed.

"What was that all about?" Violet said.

"You got me!" Jessie responded as the Aldens walked back to their bikes. "But something's definitely going on. That's for sure."

Benny, who was a few steps ahead, stopped and turned. "What do you think was in that envelope?" he asked.

"I don't know," replied Henry. "But Martin said he was counting on Auntie Two for something. I wonder what?"

"Remember what she said?" Benny asked, his voice becoming anxious. "She said, 'Soon Howard will be the only name on the door to The Underground!' "

A horrifying thought came to Jessie. "What if Martin wants the bookstore all for himself?" she said.

"Oh, Jessie!" cried Violet. "You don't really believe that, do you?"

Jessie's eyebrows drew together as she frowned. "I don't know what to believe," she said. She couldn't imagine Martin stealing Dottie's half of the business. Martin and Dottie were such close friends, that did not seem possible. But what else could Auntie Two have meant?

Benny looked over at his brother and sisters. "Should we warn Dottie?"

Henry answered first. "Let's not push the panic button yet. This is pretty suspicious, but we'd better not say anything until we have more information."

"Whatever is going on with Martin," said

Benny, "it's connected somehow to the fortune cookie mystery. I'm sure of it." He paused. Then he added, "That means there's only one thing for us to do."

The others looked at him. "What's that?" said Violet.

"Solve the fortune cookie mystery," Benny stated firmly. "And fast!"

CHAPTER 8

The Mysterious Disappearance

Aunt Jane gave the children a smile as they walked into the kitchen. "How did you make out in town?" she asked.

"You'll never guess what happened!" Benny shouted, running up and giving her a hug.

Laughing, Aunt Jane returned the hug. "What, Benny?"

"We found another fortune cookie!" he told her.

"I have to hand it to you," said Aunt Jane, looking around at them. "You children really have a way of figuring things out." She sounded proud.

"We haven't opened it yet," Henry said. "We were waiting until we got here."

Aunt Jane poured some lemonade for everyone, and the children sat down at the table. Henry broke the latest fortune cookie in half and pulled out the fortune. He stared at the little slip of paper for a moment. Then he said, "Looks like a rebus."

"A *what*?" asked Benny.

"A rebus," repeated Henry. "It's a puzzle with pictures and symbols."

"There's a hidden message in it," added Aunt Jane as she pulled up a chair. "You have to 'read' the pictures to figure out what the rebus is trying to tell you."

Henry passed the fortune to Violet. She studied the puzzle. "It looks like two ants, a cow, a bird, barbells, the number 4, and the letter U." She turned the fortune over and read aloud the message on the back. *"For an answer to a rhyme, Friday evening is the time."*

"Tomorrow's Friday!" Benny realized.

"That's true." Violet took a sip of her lemonade. The ice cubes clinked in her glass. "That doesn't give us much time to come up with an answer."

"I don't understand it," Aunt Jane said, shaking her head. "Why would someone make up all these codes and clues for you?"

"Did you check out the *i*'s?" Henry asked. "They're all dotted with little hearts again."

Jessie frowned for a moment. "I wonder what it means."

"What I don't understand is, how can you *read* pictures?" Benny said, still unsure about the rebus.

"Maybe I can show you, Benny," offered Violet. She stood up and got her sketch pad and pencils. Sitting down again, she quickly drew her own rebus. Violet was a good artist. "Can you figure this one out, Benny?" She held it up. "It's a question."

"It is?" Benny said.

Violet nodded. "When I point to each symbol, you tell me what it is."

Benny moved closer for a better look at Violet's drawing. It showed a tin can, the letter U, the letter C, and a wishing well. Benny spoke as Violet pointed. "Can . . . U . . . C . . . well. Oh! Can you see well? That's the question."

"You got it!" said Violet, clapping her hands.

"You catch on fast, Benny," Henry praised. "No wonder you're such a good detective."

"Now, let's see if we can figure out the fortune cookie rebus," suggested Jessie.

Benny was eager to give it a try. "Ants . . . cow . . . bird . . . barbells . . . 4 . . . U," he said as he looked over Jessie's shoulder. "What does *that* mean?"

Aunt Jane couldn't keep from laughing. "Doesn't make much sense, does it?"

"Well, I know one thing for sure," Benny said with a sigh. "All this detective work is making me hungry!"

"*Everything* makes you hungry, Benny!" teased Henry.

Aunt Jane smiled at her youngest nephew. "If you can wait a while longer, I'll get the barbecue going," she said. "I thought we'd have hamburgers and salad for dinner. How does that sound?"

"Sounds great!" said Benny, finishing his last sip of lemonade.

"And we'll help," said Violet, speaking for them all. The Aldens hurried away to wash up.

During dinner, the children told their aunt everything that had happened in town. "Martin Howard seems to be up to something," Jessie said as they sat around the picnic table on the back lawn. "We just don't know what."

"Auntie Two said the strangest thing," put in Violet. She remembered Auntie Two's exact words. " 'Soon Howard will be the only name on the door to The Underground.' "

Aunt Jane seemed shocked to hear this. "It's hard for me to believe that Martin would hurt Dottie," she said with a concerned look on her face. "They've always made such a great team."

"Martin said she's ruining everything. I guess that's why he doesn't want her to be part of the business anymore." Benny wiped some mustard from the corner of his mouth.

"Well, we can't be sure that's what Martin meant, Benny." Jessie helped herself to a spoonful of potato salad.

"It *is* a pretty strong case against Martin," admitted Aunt Jane. "But I hope you're not going to jump to any conclusions."

"Don't worry, Aunt Jane, we won't," Henry assured her. He knew their aunt was right. They might suspect Martin was up to no good, but they didn't have any proof. "But we're not going to rest until we solve this mystery," he added.

Benny lifted sliced tomatoes onto his plate. "I just wish we could figure out how Drum Keller fits into the whole thing."

"You mean, the famous mystery author?" Aunt Jane put down her fork. She looked startled. "The man who wrote the Fortune Cookie Mysteries?"

"Have you heard of him, Aunt Jane?" Violet asked.

"Drum Keller was one of my favorite authors. He wrote a whole series of books about a detective who keeps finding mysteries in fortune cookies. Oh!" Aunt Jane suddenly gasped. "What a strange coincidence." Her eyes widened as she looked around at them. "You children found a mystery in a fortune cookie, too!"

"What else do you know about Drum Keller?" asked Henry.

Aunt Jane took a sip of her iced tea. "I remember how shocked I was when Drum Keller disappeared."

"Disappeared?" the Aldens echoed in unison.

Nodding, Aunt Jane said, "It was almost as if he vanished into thin air."

Henry was baffled. "But he couldn't just . . . vanish!"

"Apparently he did, Henry," insisted Aunt Jane. "That was about fifteen years ago. And as far as I know, he stopped writing books and hasn't been heard from since."

"I can't believe it!" said Violet.

Henry spoke up. "Remember that customer in The Underground? Didn't he mention a mysterious disappearance?"

Benny looked over at his aunt as she dished up the fruit salad. "But . . . exactly *why* did Drum Keller vanish, Aunt Jane?"

"Some people think his disappearance was all about money," she told him. "But nobody knows for sure."

"Now I'm really confused," Benny said. "What did money have to do with it?"

"Well, it was rumored that Drum Keller wanted more money for his books. When the publishing company refused, he decided to quit writing and — "

"Disappear," finished Henry.

Aunt Jane nodded. "And when he did, he left behind a lot of disappointed readers. His mysteries were always very popular."

Jessie shook her head slowly. "It just doesn't make sense."

"Nothing about this mystery makes sense," said Henry.

Later that evening, the children sat out on Aunt Jane's front porch. They discussed the case while they watched the stars come out. "I can't stop thinking about Drum Keller," said Violet. "Why would a famous author decide to just vanish?"

Jessie sighed. "We have so many questions. And so few answers. We still have no idea who's behind this fortune cookie hunt."

"Or the reason for it," put in Benny.

"That's true," said Henry. "But there's somebody else we might want to include on our list of suspects."

"Who is it?" Violet and Benny asked at the same time.

"Drum Keller," Henry said.

Jessie, Violet, and Benny were so surprised, all they could do was stare at their older brother.

Then Violet spoke up. "You think Drum Keller wrote those weird fortunes, Henry?"

"Could be." Henry leaned forward in his chair. "Isn't he the author of a whole series of fortune cookie mysteries? And didn't we find the strange messages inside fortune cookies?"

Everyone agreed Henry had a point. It

would be easy for a mystery writer to make up codes and clues.

All of a sudden, Jessie said, "Do you realize what this means? Drum Keller might be living right here in Elmford!"

"He would have changed his name, of course. He might even be someone we know," Violet said in an awestruck voice. After a moment's thought, she added, "But why do *we* keep getting the mysterious messages?"

"Because we're detectives. We already decided that," Benny reminded her.

Henry spoke slowly, as if uncertain about what he was saying. "I can't help wondering if the messages in the fortune cookies were never meant for us at all."

Jessie looked puzzled. So did Violet and Benny.

"Think about it for a minute," Henry instructed. "Where was the first message hidden? Wasn't it inside *Dottie's* fortune cookie?" he said, answering his own question.

"It was a special cookie for the birthday

girl," recalled Benny. "But Dottie gave it to me."

"And that's not all," Henry went on. "Dottie goes to the Elmford Ice Cream Parlor every week. And she *always* gets the mystery flavor."

"That's right!" Violet cried in surprise. Her mind was racing. "Benny and Dottie both ordered the mystery flavor at about the same time. Maybe the ice-cream cones got switched around."

This got Jessie thinking. "Now that you mention it, even the *cellar* clue led us right to The Underground, where Dottie works."

Violet said what they all were thinking. "So the messages were meant for Dottie, not for us."

"We just keep getting them by mistake," realized Benny. He thought for a moment, then he added, "That reminds me of what Martin said to Auntie Two. Remember him saying, 'I don't want any more mix-ups'?"

"That's right," said Jessie. "And he wasn't very happy when Dottie gave away her special fortune cookie on her birthday."

"He stopped smiling," Benny remembered. "We thought he was just in a bad mood that day."

"Then . . . maybe *Martin's* the one who left those messages for Dottie," suggested Violet.

Jessie said, "That's an interesting theory, but . . . why would he do such a thing?"

No one had an answer to that.

"No, I still think Drum Keller's behind everything," argued Henry.

"Unless . . ." A sudden thought came to Violet.

"Unless what?" Benny questioned.

Violet's eyes were huge. "Unless Martin Howard *is* Drum Keller!"

CHAPTER 9

Spies Everywhere!

The next afternoon, Henry, Jessie, Violet, and Benny took a break from puzzling over the rebus clue. After swimming in the pond near their aunt's house, they sat in their bathing suits near the water's edge and talked about the mystery. "You really think Martin's the famous author?" Benny was saying. He held out his cracked pink cup while Violet poured lemonade from a big thermos.

"I don't really know, Benny," Violet said. "It's just a guess."

"That would explain why Martin got so upset at the bookstore," Henry said. "You know, when the customer said Drum Keller's mysteries weren't worth the paper they're printed on."

Violet nodded. "It would also explain Martin's comment at the coffee shop. When he was on the phone, I mean."

"What did he say again?" Benny looked confused.

Violet smiled at her little brother. "He said, 'Don't forget, you're dealing with Drum Keller.' "

Benny nodded. "Now I remember." He paused and frowned. "I wonder who was on the other end of the phone."

"I haven't the slightest idea." Violet tucked the thermos into her backpack. "This whole Drum Keller mystery is very odd."

Jessie sat quietly, thinking hard. She wrapped her arms around her knees. Something about the name Drum Keller was still bothering her, but she couldn't figure out what.

Benny took a big gulp, polishing off his lemonade. "If Martin *is* Drum Keller, why is he leaving these fortunes for Dottie?"

Henry dipped his toes into the cool water. "Maybe to keep her busy," he guessed. "You know, distract her so she won't notice that he's trying to steal her half of the bookstore."

Benny nodded as he crunched into an apple.

Henry continued with his theory. "People think Drum Keller disappeared because of money," he reminded them. "If Martin *is* Drum Keller, then money's very important to him."

"So Martin, also known as Drum Keller, is trying to steal Dottie's half of the bookstore so he can make more money?" Violet asked. "But . . . why is Auntie Two helping him?"

The Aldens were silent. No one had an answer.

Jessie spoke up. "There's another possibility."

Benny was instantly curious. "What is it, Jessie?"

"Maybe there is somebody else who knows the truth about Martin," she said. "Somebody who's trying to warn Dottie." Jessie pushed her damp hair behind her ears. "Maybe *that* person is leaving the strange messages."

"Oh, I hadn't thought of that," Violet exclaimed.

It made sense. What better way to hint at Martin's secret identity than by hiding a mystery in a fortune cookie? After all, Drum Keller wrote a whole series of fortune cookie mysteries, didn't he?

"Then it's *got* to be Lucy who left those messages," put in Benny, who was still convinced the waitress was behind everything. "She was talking to Angela at the ice cream parlor about somebody's secret identity. Remember? Maybe Lucy and Auntie Two are trying to warn Dottie about Martin."

"I have a hunch we won't know what's really going on," Jessie said, "until we figure out the rebus puzzle." Reaching for her backpack, she dug into a zippered pocket and pulled out the little white slip of paper.

"Maybe it'll make sense this time," Benny said hopefully.

They took turns studying the fortune again — first Violet, then Benny, then Henry, and finally Jessie. On the second time around, Violet noticed something. "I'm no expert," she said, "but I think the bird in this drawing is supposed to be a loon."

The others crowded around to take another look. "What makes you think so, Violet?" asked Jessie.

"Well, for one thing, check out the bill — it's dark and pointed." Violet had an artist's eye for detail. "And look at the white stripes on the neck."

"Good detective work, Violet," said Henry.

"But how does a loon fit in with the other drawings?" Benny wanted to know.

"I think I have that figured out," Jessie said with a big smile. "If you put the pictures of the cow and the loon together, you get—"

"Kowloon!" everyone cried out in unison.

The children looked at one another, their faces glowing with excitement. Then Benny suddenly caught his breath. "Auntie Two!" he cried. "I bet that's what the drawing of the two ants is all about."

"Good thinking, Benny." Henry gave his little brother a pat on the back. "Looks like the rebus is telling us something about Auntie Two Kowloon."

"But . . . what?" Violet wondered.

"Let's take it one drawing at a time," Henry suggested. "We figured out the first part of the rebus. Now let's study the rest of it."

Jessie frowned a moment. "The barbells come next." She pointed to the miniature drawing.

"And then the number 4," added Benny. "And the letter U."

Violet grinned. "That's the easy part, Benny," she told him. "4U means *for you.*"

Benny gave his forehead a smack. "Why didn't *I* think of that?"

"But what about the barbells?" wondered Jessie.

"Hmm." Henry tapped his chin thoughtfully. "People lift weights to build muscles."

"Oh, Henry!" cried Violet. "That's it!"

"What?"

"The rebus is saying, 'Auntie Two Kowloon *waits* for you'!"

The Aldens sat in stunned silence for a moment. Had they come full circle? Were the clues leading them back to the Kowloon Restaurant, where the mystery had started?

"What now?" Benny asked the others.

There was a long silence. Finally, Henry spoke up.

"Let's find out what this is all about," he said, pulling himself to his feet.

"How will we find out?" asked Benny.

"I think it's time to ask Auntie Two a few questions."

Everyone agreed Henry's idea was a good one. "Aunt Jane has some errands to run in town," Jessie remembered. "I'm sure she won't mind if we tag along."

Aunt Jane didn't mind at all. After an early dinner of cold chicken, corn on the cob, and leftover potato salad, they set off for Elmford. "Maybe the solution to this mystery is very simple," Aunt Jane suggested as they turned onto the highway. "Maybe it's just a game. You know, a way to entertain customers."

"You mean a sales gimmick?" Benny asked.

"Exactly," said Aunt Jane, looking surprised that Benny knew about sales gimmicks. "Maybe it's just a way for Auntie Two to attract customers."

The Aldens were quiet for a while as they considered this. Finally, Henry said, "No, this isn't just a sales gimmick, Aunt Jane. There's more to it than that." He sounded very sure.

Aunt Jane slowed the car to a stop in the parking lot.

"Don't worry, Aunt Jane," Benny said,

scrambling out of the car. "We'll get to the bottom of this mystery. Right, Henry?"

"You bet," Henry said. Then he added honestly, "At least, we'll do our best."

Aunt Jane glanced at her watch. "I'll get my errands done, then join you at the Kowloon Restaurant," she said, then hurried away in the opposite direction. The children quickly made their way to Main Street.

While they waited at the corner for the light to change, Benny asked the others, "What do you think the fortune means about an answer to a rhyme?"

Jessie threw up her hands. "That's a good question, Benny."

Violet recited the words on the fortune aloud. *"For an answer to a rhyme,/ Friday evening is the time."*

"Well, it's Friday evening," Henry pointed out as they drew near the Kowloon Restaurant. "Maybe the answer isn't far away."

Jessie nodded. "I have a feeling Drum Keller isn't far away, either." They all went inside.

At the doorway to the crowded dining

room, the Aldens stopped in surprise. "Isn't that Dottie and Martin?" asked Benny. His brother and sisters nodded.

Sure enough, the owners of The Underground were sitting at a table in the corner. The children quickly stepped out of sight. "Don't you think that's strange?" Benny demanded, his hands on his hips. "They were just here a few nights ago."

"Well, it *is* Dottie's favorite restaurant," Violet pointed out. "And isn't this the night of the concert? Maybe Dottie and Martin stopped in for a bite to eat first."

Jessie peeked around the doorway again, trying not to stare. She didn't like the idea of spying on anyone. In this case, though, she felt they were doing it for a good cause. "Look at Auntie Two over there. She's watching Dottie and Martin from behind that potted plant." Everyone looked.

Violet's eyebrows shot up. "What's that all about?"

"I don't know," said Benny. "But she's close enough to hear everything they're saying."

"If you think that's odd," Jessie added in a hushed voice, "Lucy seems to be keeping a close eye on them, too."

They all looked over to where the young woman in the white apron was dashing from table to table, taking orders and refilling water glasses. Every few seconds she would glance at the table in the corner where Dottie and Martin were deep in conversation.

The Aldens turned to one another in bewilderment. It seemed as if the more they watched, the more confusing it became. Before they could begin to figure out what was happening, Violet said, "Look! Martin just signaled to Auntie Two."

The children stared at Auntie Two as she stepped out from behind the potted plant and walked straight to the table in the corner. The owner of the Kowloon Restaurant held out a small plate with a fortune cookie on it. Smiling, Dottie reached out, broke the fortune cookie in half, and removed the little white slip of paper.

Benny grabbed Jessie's hand when Dottie cried out, "Oh—oh, my!"

CHAPTER 10

An Answer to a Rhyme

"He did it!" Benny exclaimed. "Martin stole Dottie's half of the bookstore. I just know it!"

"What can we do?" Violet asked in alarm.

"I'm not sure," said Jessie. "But we have to do *something*. Right, Henry?"

Henry didn't answer. He was staring into the dining room, watching Martin remove a small velvet box from his jacket pocket.

"Wait!" Henry said. "Isn't that the box from the jewelry store? The one the sales-clerk tried to show Martin?"

The others followed Henry's gaze.

"Martin said he was looking at watches," Benny remembered. "But that box is too small for a watch."

Suddenly, Henry understood. "What if Martin wasn't looking at watches at all?" he said slowly. "What if he was *really* at the jewelry store looking at something else?"

"Like what, Henry?" asked Violet.

"Like a diamond ring!" Henry answered.

"Oh, Henry!" Violet put a hand over her mouth in surprise. "You think Martin's asking Dottie to marry him?"

"I can't be sure," Henry admitted. "But it's possible."

"You could be right, Henry," Jessie realized. "The rings and the watches were in the same display case."

"And that would explain what Auntie Two meant about *one* name on the door to The Underground!" said Violet. She sounded excited.

Benny looked confused. "I don't get it."

Violet smiled at her little brother. "If Dottie and Martin get married, then Dottie's name will be Howard, too. So Howard *will* be the only name on the door!"

Benny's eyes widened. "Dottie and Martin are getting married?"

"Let's find out," suggested Henry. Without another word, he led the way across the crowded dining room to Martin and Dottie's table.

"The Aldens!" Auntie Two greeted the children with a smile. She looked surprised to see them. So did Martin and Dottie.

"You're just in time to hear what my fortune says," Dottie told them, her eyes shining. She read aloud the words on the little slip of paper:

> *"In a fortune cookie,*
> *A question hides:*
> *Dottie, will you be my bride?"*

"Oh, a proposal in a fortune cookie!" Violet clasped her hands. "How romantic!"

Martin gave Dottie a questioning look. "I still don't have an answer to my rhyme."

"Of course I'll marry you, Martin!" cried Dottie, blinking back the tears.

The Aldens looked at one another. That's what the fortune meant about an answer to a rhyme!

Martin opened the small velvet box. Inside was a sparkling diamond ring! Without a word, he slipped the ring onto Dottie's finger.

As the Aldens and Auntie Two laughed and clapped their hands, Lucy arrived with a beautiful heart-shaped cake edged with pink roses made of sugar. The lettering on top read: DOTTIE AND MARTIN FOREVER. And the *i*'s were dotted with candy hearts.

"My goodness! Another surprise!" Dottie exclaimed as Lucy set the cake on the table. "Did you plan this, too, Martin?"

He shook his head. "Noooo . . . but I can guess who did."

Lucy laughed. "It was teamwork. Auntie Two did the baking, and I did the decorating."

Dottie smiled over at Lucy and Auntie Two. "So you were both in on this, were you?"

"From the beginning," confessed Auntie Two. "Martin gave me his rhyming proposal yesterday, and I made a very special fortune cookie to put it in. I could hardly stand the suspense waiting for Martin's okay to bring that fortune cookie over. I just knew you'd say yes!" she added.

The Aldens looked at one another. Now they knew what was in the envelope Martin had given Auntie Two — it was the fortune cookie proposal.

"I've been holding my breath, too," Lucy confided. "I was just waiting for my cue to bring out the cake."

"I can't help wondering who else was in on this," Dottie said, smiling happily.

Jessie knew the answer to that one. "Angela helped, too, right?"

"Right," responded Martin. "She played a very important part in my little game."

"She sure did," Henry realized. "Angela invented Fortune Cookie Delight!"

"Right again," said Martin, gesturing for the four Aldens to sit down. "Please join the celebration."

Benny didn't need to be coaxed. "This explains what you were doing in the jewelry store, Martin," he said as everyone pulled up a chair.

Violet added, "You seemed so eager to get away from us."

"I'm sorry about that, Violet," apologized Martin. "I was afraid you'd find out I was looking at engagement rings. I knew if Dottie smelled anything fishy going on, it would ruin the surprise."

"We didn't figure it out for a while," admitted Benny. "At first, we thought you were trying to steal Dottie's half of the bookstore."

"You thought I was a thief?" Martin asked in surprise.

Dottie laughed a little. "Martin *did* steal my heart. But that was his only crime."

"I bet I can solve a mystery, too," Lucy said as she dished up the cake.

"What mystery?" Benny wanted to know.

"The mystery of why you're here," she said. Her lips curled into a little smile. "You

children don't give up. You've been following the fortune cookie clues, haven't you?"

"You should know," answered Henry,
watching the waitress closely. "After all,
they were *your* invention. Right, Lucy?"

"How did you know?" the waitress asked
in surprise.

Henry pointed to the cake. "You dotted
the *i*'s on the cake with candy hearts," he
pointed out. "The *i*'s in the fortune cookie
messages were dotted with hearts, too."

"Oh, dear!" Lucy laughed a little. "I certainly gave myself away, didn't I?"

"The messages really were meant for
Dottie," said Violet. "Weren't they? That's
why you added the romantic hearts."

Lucy didn't deny it. "I overheard Martin
telling Auntie Two about the special way he
wanted to propose to Dottie — by taking
her on a fortune cookie adventure." She
paused as she handed Benny his slice of
cake. "I happen to be pretty good at making up codes and clues, so I offered my ser-
vices. It's my dream to become a mystery

writer, you know. Just like my favorite author — Drum Keller. I just love The Fortune Cookie Mysteries! Anyway," she said, smiling a little, "that's how I got involved in this whole fortune cookie business. Unfortunately, it didn't go as smoothly as I'd planned. The cookies kept ending up with the four of you instead."

Violet nodded in understanding. Lucy was the one Martin had been blaming for ruining everything.

"Now, don't feel badly, Lucy," Dottie said kindly. "I was the one who insisted Benny open the first fortune cookie. And I wouldn't take no for an answer."

"That's true," said Martin. "Why, Auntie Two even accused *me* of botching things up that night. She thought I might be getting cold feet."

Jessie and Henry exchanged glances. That must have been the phone conversation they'd overheard at the coffee shop!

"Cold feet?" Benny was wrinkling his face. "What does that mean?"

"That means having second thoughts about proposing to Dottie," explained Martin. "Of course, I wasn't having second thoughts at all. But after all the mix-ups, I *did* give up on the mystery idea."

Violet smiled as she took the cake the waitress handed her. "You know, Lucy, it wasn't your fault at the ice cream parlor, either," she pointed out. "You're not the one who got the cones mixed up."

"True," Martin agreed.

Lucy managed a weak smile. "I've been a nervous wreck all week," she said. "I wanted so much to impress you, Martin."

"*Me?*" Martin pointed to himself. Then he began to laugh. "Why would you want to impress me?"

Violet was fairly sure she knew the answer. "Because you figured out that Martin is Drum Keller. Right, Lucy?"

The waitress looked questioningly at Martin. "Is it true? Are you the famous author?"

It was obvious by the look on Martin's face that he was shocked. "Why, no!"

Lucy looked surprised — and disappointed.

The Aldens were every bit as surprised as Lucy. They were so sure Drum Keller was someone they knew. And their hunches were usually right.

Benny was wondering about something else. He hesitated for a minute, then blurted out, "Why did you run away from us at the ice cream parlor, Lucy?"

After a brief silence, Lucy said, "The truth is, I was afraid you'd ask me a lot of questions about that fortune cookie. So I kept my distance."

"Only you changed your mind and followed us, didn't you?" said Henry.

Lucy looked embarrassed. "Yes, I did follow you," she acknowledged. "I wanted to find out if you got Dottie's fortune cookie by mistake again."

Jessie nodded. "I *felt* someone watching us."

"I'm sorry if I frightened you," Lucy apologized. "I guess I wasn't thinking straight."

Henry turned to Martin. "Something puzzles me, too."

"What is it?" Martin took a sip of water.

"If you gave up on the mystery idea," said Henry, "then why did you leave the last fortune cookie in The Underground?"

"I simply forgot all about it, Henry." Martin shrugged a little. "I'm afraid I wasn't thinking straight, either."

Aunt Jane, who had just come up behind them, said, "What's this? A celebration of some kind?" As Aunt Jane pulled up a chair, Dottie held up her hand to show off the beautiful ring. "I just can't believe it," said Aunt Jane, smiling over at Dottie and Martin's beaming faces. "This is the best news I've heard in a long time."

Martin raised his water glass. "I'd like everyone to join me in a toast," he said. "Fifteen years ago today this fine lady left her hometown of Keller's Crossing and arrived in Elmford. Let's drink a toast to my future bride — Dorothy Ruth Ursela May!"

Jessie's jaw dropped. Everything suddenly clicked into place. "Oh, my goodness!"

she cried, putting her hands to her mouth.

The others turned to look at her. "What's the matter, Jessie?"

"I know the answer to another mystery," she told them in an awestruck voice.

"*Another* mystery?" Martin asked.

"I know who Drum Keller is," Jessie said. She looked right at Dottie Shallum.

Dottie lowered her eyes.

Benny looked confused. "But, Jessie, Drum Keller's a man. Remember?"

"That's just what we thought," Jessie told him.

Again Dottie seemed to be pretending not to hear. Even Martin was strangely quiet.

"It all fits," Jessie went on. "You came to Elmford fifteen years ago, Dottie. That's when Drum Keller disappeared."

"But Jessie — " began Violet.

"That's not all," Jessie cut in. "The first letters in Dorothy Ruth Ursela May spell — "

"DRUM!" Henry cried out, his voice rising with excitement.

Jessie nodded slowly. "And Keller is from

the name of Dottie's hometown — Keller's Crossing! That's the part that seemed familiar to me. I just couldn't remember why."

All eyes turned to Dottie. Her mouth opened, but nothing came out right away. For a long time, she didn't say a word. Finally, she smiled. "I guess you've found me out," she said. She looked around at all the faces staring at her. Then she took a deep breath and continued, "I wrote The Fortune Cookie Mystery series when I was living in Keller's Crossing. My publishers wanted to keep my identity a secret. They thought it would be a good — "

"Sales gimmick?" put in Benny.

"Exactly, Benny." Dottie patted his hand. "They thought it would be a good sales gimmick to make Drum Keller very mysterious. The whole idea suited me just fine. You see, I was never interested in fame. It was always the writing I loved."

Violet looked confused. "Then why did you suddenly stop, Dottie?"

"My husband became very ill." Dottie

looked at the children sadly. "After he died, I decided to stop writing the Drum Keller mysteries. My heart just wasn't in it, anymore."

"Dottie packed her bags," said Martin, picking up where his partner had left off, "and came to Elmford to make a fresh start."

"Martin and Auntie Two were the only ones who knew about my secret identity," Dottie continued. "The publishing company simply announced that Drum Keller had disappeared."

Jessie shot Henry a glance. No wonder Dottie wouldn't part with those books in the cabinet. She was the author! That would explain Martin's behavior, too. He was upset to hear the customer insulting Dottie's books.

"When Benny found that strange message in his fortune cookie," Dottie went on, "everything came rushing back to me. I remembered how much fun I used to have making up codes and clues."

"Is that why you wanted to sniff out some clues with us?" asked Benny.

"Yes, Benny." Dottie nodded. "I was also very curious. You see, I knew that first fortune cookie was meant for me. But I couldn't figure out *why* someone had made it."

"This is all my fault, Dottie," said Martin. He looked troubled. "I never meant to betray your secret. But how could I know the Aldens would come along and figure everything out?"

Dottie waved this away. "I'm glad the truth is out, Martin. I'm tired of keeping the past a secret." Turning to Lucy, she added, "I'd love to read some of your stories, Lucy. And who knows? Maybe I can even give you a few pointers."

"Thank you." Lucy sounded pleased. "I would love that!"

"I might even try writing another Drum Keller mystery," added Dottie. "How would you feel about that, Martin?"

"It would make me very proud," Martin replied, his voice filled with emotion.

"Will it be another mystery in a fortune cookie, Dottie?" Benny asked hopefully.

"You bet, Benny," said the famous author. "You bet!"

GERTRUDE CHANDLER WARNER discovered when she was teaching that many readers who like an exciting story could find no books that were both easy and fun to read. She decided to try to meet this need, and her first book, *The Boxcar Children*, quickly proved she had succeeded.

Miss Warner drew on her own experiences to write the mystery. As a child she spent hours watching trains go by on the tracks opposite her family home. She often dreamed about what it would be like to set up housekeeping in a caboose or freight car — the situation the Alden children find themselves in.

When Miss Warner received requests for more adventures involving Henry, Jessie, Violet, and Benny Alden, she began additional stories. In each, she chose a special setting and introduced unusual or eccentric characters who liked the unpredictable.

While the mystery element is central to each of Miss Warner's books, she never thought of them as strictly juvenile mysteries. She liked to stress the Aldens' independence and resourcefulness and their solid New England devotion to using up and making do. The Aldens go about most of their adventures with as little adult supervision as possible — something else that delights young readers.

Miss Warner lived in Putnam, Connecticut, until her death in 1979. During her lifetime, she received hundreds of letters from girls and boys telling her how much they liked her books.